Chelsey and the Green-Haired Kid

Chelsey
and the
Green-Haired Kid

by Carol Gorman

Houghton Mifflin Company
Boston   1987
    6-8

Library of Congress Cataloging in Publication Data

Gorman, Carol.
  Chelsey and the green-haired kid.

  Summary: Convinced that the fatal accident she wit-
nessed at the basketball game was not accidental,
thirteen-year-old Chelsey, a paraplegic, and her unusual
friend Jack join forces to prove it was a deliberate
murder.
  [1. Mystery and detective stories. 2. Physically
handicapped—Fiction] I. Title.
PZ7.G6693Ch 1987   [Fic]   86-20978
ISBN 0-395-41854-2

Printed in the United States of America

S 10 9 8 7 6 5 4 3 2 1

For my sister, Christy McGinty
And for the men in my life, Ed and Ben

For the silent . . . .
And to . . . .

Chelsey and the Green-Haired Kid

One

I saved the picture of Jack and me from the front page of the newspaper. I get it out sometimes and look at it, now that all the excitement has died down.

Even in a black and white photograph, we make a pretty unusual pair, me in my wheelchair, and Jack, with his closely cropped punk hair, standing with his hands stuffed easily into his pockets, smiling that little smile of his.

Not your everyday-looking heroes.

Until the night of the murder, I'd never laid eyes on Jack before. And believe me, if I'd seen him before that snowy March night, I would definitely have remembered him. Jack is not someone you can easily forget.

Then there's me. I'm Chelsey Bernard, and I'm in

the seventh grade at Lowman Middle School. Before I got famous, I was an average blond-haired, blue-eyed thirteen-year-old girl, except for my mode of transportation. I've used a wheelchair since the car accident when I was three. A lady ran a red light and plowed into my mom's little VW. My mom was okay, but I ended up with no feeling in my legs or feet. So I ride around in my wheelchair, the Blue Streak.

Anyway, I'll remember that winter night as long as I live. The Lincoln High School parking lot was jammed with the usual basketball crowd, even though the temperature was down around zero degrees and the snow was blowing so hard you could barely see the car in front of your own. The calendar read March, but it felt more like January. I guess winter was stubbornly giving us one last big blast before finally giving in to spring.

My dad was chauffeuring me in the Monster, our big, gross van that has enough room in the back for my chair.

We pulled up as close to the gymnasium door as we could, in one of the handicapped parking spaces, and I rode the hydraulic lift on the back of the van down to the ground level outside.

My dad would've escorted me inside if I'd wanted him to, but I like to do things on my own every chance I get. When you're a girl, thirteen, and handicapped, parents can practically smother you with protection if you let them. So I waved goodbye to

Dad at the door and rode into the building with a big wave of people.

Normally I go to the high school games with my friend Paula, but she had to have company for dinner, so she missed out on everything. Even though she says murder is sick and ugly, she still wishes she'd gone with me that night.

As I wheeled into the gym, the players were warming up, bouncing the balls around the court and shooting baskets. Lincoln High School has been quite a powerhouse in basketball the last several years, and the tension is always high at the games. The guys were taking these incredible shots halfway down the court and sinking them with no problem. The crowd loved it.

The players looked psyched up but confident, trotting around in their red and white uniforms, clapping their hands and swatting each other on the rear the way jocks always do.

The fans were pressing through the gym door and hurrying to find seats in the bleachers before the game started. Usually every available space is occupied in the stands, except for maybe the top back row behind the pep band.

There's a special place I like to sit during the games at the far corner of the gymnasium. I have to wheel myself around the back of all the bleachers in order to get to that spot. But because it was so crowded, I parked myself next to the inside wall to wait for the incoming crowd to dwindle down a bit before making my way back there.

By that time, the players had disappeared to the locker room for their pep talk from the coach. I wondered what Lincoln's coach was saying that could pep up the guys more than they already were. He's the kind of coach who falls to his knees and pounds the floor when our guys make a mistake. When he yells, you can see his deep red face and the veins sticking out in his neck from halfway across the gymnasium. I wished I could turn into an ant and crawl into the locker room to listen to his speech. I bet it was really something.

It was hot in the gym with so many people packed inside. I unbuttoned my coat, slipped out of it, and laid it across my lap along with my wool cap and mittens.

By the time the guys jogged back out on the basketball court, the crowd was mostly in the bleachers, so I figured I could make my way around to the other side now without getting stampeded. The pep band was playing a loud rock-song-arranged-for-pep-bands tune and the people were on their feet, clapping and cheering.

I wheeled around the back end of the bleachers. The light was dim, and at first I thought I saw someone climb under the bleacher seats, but when I looked more carefully no one was there.

4

I could see well enough to know that the path was clear all along the back of the seats. The crowd was really wild, stamping their feet and yelling over the band. I could see hundreds of feet through the back, tramping on the floor of the risers, stomping on scattered kernels of popcorn. The vibrations pulsated through my chair. The noise roared in my ears. *This is what basketball games are all about,* I thought, feeling an excited tingle climb up my back. My wheels glided easily over the smooth hardwood floor.

A sudden movement at the top of the bleachers caught my eye. I turned my attention up ahead to the back of the top row, where a large boy, maybe fifteen or sixteen years old, teetered at the top. He was sitting on the safety rail at the back of the last row behind the band. The rail had two horizontal bars and he sat with his rear on the lower bar, his head and shoulders behind the upper bar. He was holding on to the rail with one hand. I took all of this in in maybe half a second, and as I glanced up, he suddenly lunged backward as if he'd been shoved. He wildly made a grab to catch himself, but it was too late. I heard myself scream as his body plunged to the floor. He landed with a thud. Even through the noise of the band and the crowd, I heard the sound of his body hit the wood. It was awful.

He lay still about twenty feet from me.

I glanced up at the top of the bleachers where he'd

fallen from. A guy about seventeen or so moved quickly along the top row. He glanced over the edge, first at the boy on the floor, and then at me.

A long, hard look at me. With hard, dark eyes. Then his head disappeared.

At that moment, I realized what I'd seen. Or almost seen.

Somebody had tried to kill the boy.

Two

For a moment, I sat there frozen. I didn't know what to do.

The crowd was still cheering the team on the court but beginning to settle down a little. No one else had noticed the boy fall.

I inched my chair closer to the unmoving boy on the floor. His blue parka was unzipped and lay open around him, the bright orange lining framing his body. His arms were stretched out at his sides. A pair of dark-rimmed glasses lay broken and twisted at his feet.

It was too dimly lit for me to see him, to know if he was breathing or not. I couldn't imagine how he would survive a fall like that, hitting the floor the way he did.

But I wasn't about to make that judgment by myself. I spun my wheelchair around and whisked my way back the way I'd come, trying to find somebody to help. Maybe the boy wasn't dead yet and fast action could save his life.

I spotted a small crowd of high school kids as I rounded the edge of the bleachers.

"Come quick!" I yelled to them. "A guy's hurt back here!"

A couple of the students turned to stare at me quizzically.

"Please!" I yelled again. "Please help him! He fell off the bleachers!"

"What?"

"Some kid fell?"

"Someone's hurt?"

The kids glanced at each other and back at me. Then the whole group, about six boys and girls, hurried toward me.

"Who is it?"

"Get help! Call an ambulance!"

Their excited voices and scurrying steps drew the attention of more people, and in less than a minute the boy was surrounded by a small crowd.

"Does anyone know this boy?" a man asked, taking charge right away. He looked into the boy's eyes and felt the vein in his neck, checking for a pulse. He started pushing on the boy's chest with short, quick thrusts, and giving him mouth-to-mouth resuscitation.

"Is he dead?" someone asked.

The man didn't even glance up or break rhythm with his CPR. "Just about," he murmured between breaths.

Kids in the crowd pushed to see him.

"Who is he?"

"I never saw him before."

"I think he's in my homeroom."

"No, I don't think he goes to Lincoln. Does he have an ID?"

People were pushing in around him, and I could barely see him anymore.

Curious spectators at the game peeked through the bleachers to see what all the commotion was about. Others stood in the top row, watching from the spot where the boy'd fallen from.

I was surprised how fast the ambulance and police arrived. By now, there were so many people standing around behind the bleachers that I couldn't see the boy at all. So I just sat at the side of the crowd and waited.

I wasn't sure what I was waiting for. I wanted to tell someone that the boy didn't just *fall*, that he was pushed. But there was so much noise and confusion, and I didn't know just who to talk to.

The ambulance attendants pushed their way

through the crowd wheeling a low bed on wheels. They disappeared for a few minutes, and then emerged from the crowd, rolling the boy quickly along the floor and whisking him out the door.

Five or six policemen in blue uniforms helped control the crowd of people, while several others, scribbling in little notebooks, began talking to the spectators who were milling around the floor.

Now was my chance to tell them what I'd seen.

I pivoted my chair around and headed for the nearest police officer. He was talking with one of the boys I'd yelled to right after the kid fell. The boy turned and saw me coming, and he said, "There she is! That's the girl who saw it."

The cop glanced at me, nodded to the boy to dismiss him, and then turned again in my direction. He tapped his cap in a sort of polite little salute. "Evenin', young lady," the officer said. "You see it happen?"

"Yessir," I said. "It was awful."

"I can imagine," he said, nodding. "He fell from quite a height. What was he doing, balancing on the rail?"

"No," I said, "he was just sitting on the lower rail. But" — I paused to be sure he'd get this important part — "he didn't just fall by himself."

"He didn't?"

"No," I said quite emphatically. "He was pushed."

The policeman's eyes widened a little in the dim light. "He was pushed? Did you see someone push him?"

"Not exactly," I began. "But I'm sure someone did. He jerked back as if someone right in front of him shoved him backward really hard."

"But you didn't actually see it happen?"

"No," I said, "but I did see a guy look over the rail just after the kid fell. He looked at the boy on the floor and then at me."

"Yes?" the officer said.

"Then he disappeared. He got out of there pretty fast."

"Did you see this guy touch the boy before he fell?"

I thought he'd already asked me that question. I guess he was just being thorough.

"No, sir," I said. "But I know the guy had something to do with it."

"How do you know that?" the officer said.

I paused. How do you explain that you can tell things like that just by looking into someone's eyes? I could tell by the way he stared over the edge of the rail at the boy, and how he glared at me. But somehow, it wasn't going to sound right when I told the policeman about that. About his eyes.

"Just the way he looked, I guess," I said feebly, glancing away because I felt embarrassed about not being able to explain. Something under a lower bleacher seat caught my eye. Kind of a shadow, which caught the light just then and glimmered green. Probably someone's scarf dropped from an upper seat, I figured.

"Well," the policeman sighed, taking a step back. "Thank you for giving me this information. I'm afraid that if you didn't actually see anyone push the boy, there isn't much we can do."

I felt my heart sink, and I guess he saw what that feeling did to my face, because he said, "Why don't you give me a description of the guy on the bleachers who stared at you? I'll add it to the report. Maybe someone else saw the boy shoved, and if so, we can go from there."

"Okay." I swallowed. "I just saw him for a couple of seconds. But he was old. Much older."

"How old would you guess?" the policeman asked.

"At least seventeen or eighteen," I said.

"I see. Yes, much older." The officer smiled and wrote on his pad.

"And he had very dark eyes. And dark hair."

"Build?"

"Not tall and not short. Sort of medium. And he wore a red stocking cap, and his hair was curly and stuck out from under the cap, all around."

"What color was his coat?" he asked, still writing.

"Uhm. I'm not sure. Dark," I said.

"Okay. Anything else?" He looked up from the paper.

"I guess not," I said.

"Okay, young lady, why don't I get your name and address, and I guess that'll wrap it up."

My insides felt hard and twisted. I gave him the information about who I was in case they needed to ask more questions, but I could tell the policeman didn't think he'd be talking to me again. That meant that no one would investigate the older boy or the pushing, unless someone had seen it. And that meant that a boy might die and his murderer would go free.

The police officer flipped his notepad closed.

"Okay, Chelsey," he said. "If you think of anything else, give us a call down at the station. I'm Detective Evans."

"Okay, I will," I said. "I hope the boy is all right, and I hope you catch the guy who pushed him."

"Yes. A terrible acci —— a terrible tragedy." He touched his cap again with a sad little tap and strolled away into the lighted doorway of the gymnasium.

The darkness closed in around me, sitting there in back of the bleachers. Most of the fans were back at the game. Only a few stragglers stood in the shadows at the far wall.

The darkness was cool and peaceful and somehow felt soothing to my raw nerves. I wasn't ready to wheel myself into the bright fluorescent lights at the other end of the bleachers. And I wasn't in the mood for basketball.

So when the voice came out of nowhere, it really startled me.

"So what are ya going to do now?"

I jumped a little. I glanced around quickly but didn't see anyone.

"What?" I asked, almost involuntarily.

"What are ya going to do? The cop didn't believe you."

I turned in the direction of the voice. The same spot where I'd seen the green scarf. Someone was standing in the shadows under the bleachers.

I squinted to get a better look. He moved a little. That green again. But it didn't look like a scarf.

Then he stepped out from under the bleachers.

"I couldn't help overhearing your conversation," he said with a small smile.

"What were you doing under there?" I asked.

"Watching the game, just like everyone else," he said, continuing to smile.

"I've never heard of anyone watching a game from *under* the bleachers," I said, pointedly.

"You've never met me." The boy shrugged, still smiling a little.

That was true. I'd sure never seen this kid before. I peered closer at him in the dim light.

"You've got green hair," I said.

"You've got blue eyes," he said, without missing a beat.

He continued to stand there, smiling faintly, swaying just a little from side to side. Almost like a snake charmer.

Other than the green hair, which was cropped closely to his head, he looked like any other kid. No, that isn't quite right. On the *outside*, he looked like any other kid, wearing blue jeans and a dark tee shirt. Other than the fact that he wore no coat, he was dressed just like most of the other eighth- or ninth-grade boys.

But there was something different about him — something very different. And again, it's hard to describe, because it was all in the eyes. The way he just stood there looking at me, smiling just a little, with his eyes locked into mine, made him seem older or worldly or something that I didn't understand.

To tell you the truth, I'd never had a boy look at me that way before, and it was wonderful and embarrassing, both at the same time. There were butterflies in my stomach, and I could've sworn my heart was beating double-time.

I tore my eyes away from his to get out from under the spell he was casting.

"So what were you doing eavesdropping on my

conversation with the policeman?" I asked a little sharply, wanting him to think his charm wasn't working on me.

"Like I told you, I was just watching the game, Chelsey," he said, shrugging.

"Well, you heard enough to get my name," I said.

"So I'll tell you mine, and then we'll be even," he said. "The name is Jack. Jack Smith."

"Sounds like you made it up," I said.

His smile widened. "Not only cute, but a wiseass, too," he said. "I like that. You got a lot of spunk for someone riding around in a wheelchair."

That made me mad. "So what's my chair got to do with anything?" I said angrily. "My chair isn't me. *I'm* me! I just don't happen to be able to walk and use my legs the way you do. I mean, coming from somebody with green hair, that's a pretty weird thing to say."

He stared at me seriously for a long moment without saying anything, just swaying in that funny way. Then he nodded slightly. "See you around, Chelsey."

Then he turned away from me and sauntered toward the door.

"Hey, wait a minute!" I called after him.

He stopped in his tracks and slowly turned.

"You saw the boy fall, didn't you?" I asked.

"I didn't see a thing," Jack said, locking eyes with me again.

"Yes, you did. I saw you in here just before he was pushed. You climbed under the bleachers when you saw me coming, just before the boy fell. That's why you were listening to my conversation with the officer."

"I never saw a thing," he repeated. Then he casually thrust his hands into his pockets, turned, and strolled out the door.

Three

"Did you hear about the accident at the game?" Paula grabbed my arm as I opened my locker.

"Yeah, I was there," I said.

"Really?" Paula stared at me astonished. "You saw the cops and everything?"

Paula had found yet another way to fix her hair. One side was combed up and over the top of her head so that it hung down partway on the other side. A sparkly barrette held the hair in place.

To tell you the truth, she looked pretty lopsided.

"Yeah. I saw the kid fall," I said, tossing my math book into the bottom of my locker.

"You saw it *happen*, even?" Paula looked impressed. "You were behind the bleachers?"

She scrambled to the other side of my chair. I

could tell she was going to want all the details.

"Yeah," I said, reaching to the upper shelf of my locker for my English book. "Paula, hand me my lit book, will you? I don't know why they have to make these shelves so high."

"So tell me how it happened!" she said, thrusting my lit book at me.

"He fell off the back," I said simply. "I don't know who he was. I hope he's okay. He really smacked the floor hard."

I turned around and stuffed the book into the canvas bag attached to the back of my chair.

"Haven't you heard?" Paula said, her eyes big. "He died. Right after they got him to the hospital. Didn't you hear? It was on the news Saturday night."

"He died?" I said, my throat tightening. "Oh, no."

"Sure did," she said.

"Did you hear who he was?" I asked.

"His name was Jerry Fields. I think he was a sophomore at Lincoln. He worked down at Mac's making deliveries."

Mac's is a pizza joint, one of the hangouts where you can count on seeing maybe fifty percent of the high school kids in town on any given weekend. They make a great taco pizza, my favorite.

Right now I wasn't thinking of taco pizza, though. My mind was replaying the scene behind the bleachers three nights before, when Jerry Fields fell to his death. No, was *pushed*. Was *pushed* to his death.

It felt kind of strange to have a name for the boy now. Jerry Fields. Now he was a whole person in my mind, with a name, an identity. I even knew where he'd worked. I couldn't stand apart from him in my mind anymore.

At first, I was going to tell Paula that I'd seen someone push Jerry. But, knowing Paula, it'd be all over school in five minutes. And since I didn't have proof, and since I don't especially like drawing attention to myself, I decided to wait.

Maybe someone else who saw the mysterious older kid push Jerry will come forward, I thought. *Until then, I'll keep it a secret.*

"Did you talk to the cops?" Paula asked, walking beside me as we headed toward our English class. "Did you tell them you saw him fall?"

"Yes," I said. "I told them how it all happened. I was the only one there."

"Wow," she murmured.

Jerry Fields's accident was practically the only topic of conversation at school all morning. A lot of the kids said they'd seen him going in and out of Mac's Pizza, or that he'd come to their houses making his deliveries. Everyone said he'd seemed kind of nice, but maybe a little nerdy, and very quiet. He'd been on the pudgy side and worn thick, dark-rimmed glasses that always slid down his nose. He'd bring a pizza to your door, hand it to you, take your money, make change, and leave, all without saying more than two words.

Why would anyone want to kill a person like that? Usually people who are murdered on TV and in mysteries are creeps, and there are always thousands of suspects, all with very good reasons for wanting the victim to die.

Say a tyrant boss is making life miserable for his employees, firing some people and threatening others, and he's cheating on his wife besides and maybe even kicking his dog. Then one day he's found dead, floating in his swimming pool. Immediately, you can suspect all of his employees, his wife, his girlfriend, and any animal lover who happened to see him give his dog a boot.

But this case was different. Jerry seemed to be a nice, ordinary kid. Not a guy who could provoke someone to murder him.

Unless maybe he wasn't the nice guy everyone believed he was, and he had a secret life no one knew about, I thought as I picked up my tray in the cafeteria at lunch.

After paying the cashier, I balanced my tray across the arms of my wheelchair and slowly made my way to my usual table at the back of the lunchroom, away from the jostling crowd and next to the wall.

I slid my tray onto the end of the long table and maneuvered the Blue Streak into place. Paula was late for lunch as usual. She always comes flying in ten minutes late, which means that she has exactly twelve minutes to pick up her lunch and wolf down her food before we have to get back to class.

I looked at my lunch. Macaroni and cheese. Not exactly one of my favorites, especially the way the school cooks make it. Mushy with no flavor.

I was lifting a forkful of it toward my mouth when I glanced up and saw Jack Smith across the cafeteria. He wasn't easy to miss, being the only kid with green hair. He'd just strolled through the doorway as if he owned the place.

He quickly scanned the room, and his eyes stopped on me. I smiled, then quickly looked away, feeling my face getting hot. And I hate to admit it, but the fork in my right hand with macaroni and cheese on it was trembling just a little. It was the first time I'd ever been nervous about seeing a boy.

Within a minute he stood beside me.

"Is that stuff really edible, Chels?" he asked.

"Chels?" I put down my fork and stared at him. No one, I mean *no one* calls me Chels.

"Yeah, is that good?" He carried no books and his hands were stuffed into his pockets. He tilted his head to the side slightly and watched me intently.

"Nothing else was on the menu," I said.

He nodded and smiled a little but said nothing.

"Aren't you going to eat?" I asked.

"Not hungry," he answered.

"Then would you stop staring at me?" I asked. "It's hard to eat when someone's watching every bite."

"You like this place, Chelsey?" he asked, looking around the cafeteria.

"It's all right," I said. "The food's pretty bad, but —"

"No," Jack stopped me. "The school." He was staring at me again.

"It's okay," I said.

This guy had a strange way of making conversation. Asking dumb questions while staring straight through me. It made me feel uncomfortable.

"Want to split?" he asked, not batting an eye.

"What? You mean leave school? Now?"

He shrugged. "Why not?"

For a second, I couldn't answer. I mean, no one in my life had ever suggested leaving school in the middle of the day. Maybe not going in the first place, but not just waltzing out the door after lunch.

"Because." I couldn't look at him.

There was a moment of silence.

"Because why?" he asked.

"I've never played hooky," I said. "I'd rather not be at school, but I'm not going to leave."

I pushed the macaroni around my plate.

There was a long pause. I still didn't look at him.

"Chelsey," he said.

"What?" I concentrated on my fork.

He didn't say anything. There was another long pause.

When I finally glanced up at him, he had that small smile on his face.

"What's so funny?" I asked him, feeling my face getting hotter. "Why do you keep smiling like that? What do you want?"

"What do you mean?" he asked.

"I mean, you ask me to leave school with you right in the middle of the day. I don't even know you. All I know is your name is Jack Smith. The only time I ever saw you before was when a boy was pushed off the bleachers at Lincoln High School, and you came out from under the bleachers after eavesdropping on my conversation with the police officer. And you *claimed* you didn't see it happen."

Jack had stopped smiling and was staring at me with his back straight and stiff, as if he'd been nailed to a board.

"Did you?" I asked, narrowing my eyes and staring right back. Suddenly I wasn't nervous anymore. I wanted to get to the bottom of this.

"Did I what?" His chin was set hard and I saw the muscles tighten in his jaw.

"Did you see Jerry Fields fall." I said it like a statement, not a question, never taking my eyes from him.

"I told you before, Chelsey," he said slowly and evenly, "I didn't see anything."

"Look, I need some help," I said. "I saw someone

up there with Jerry just after he fell. I *know* he was pushed. If you saw *anything* before you climbed under the bleachers —"

"Chelsey," he said quietly. "You're wasting your time. I can't help you."

There was a long pause while we tried to stare each other down.

Hurried footsteps right behind me broke the tension.

"Wow, am I ever late this time!" Paula plopped down on the bench next to my chair. "Yuck, mac and cheese, I hate it."

She stopped, suddenly aware that she'd come in on the middle of something. "Oh, sorry, did I interrupt?" She looked at me and then at Jack, then back at me again.

"S'all right," Jack said. "I was just leaving." He nodded to me with a grim look, turned, and walked off.

"Who was *that?*" Paula asked. "His hair's green."

"Jack Smith," I said.

"He new?" Paula asked. "I've never seen him before."

"I guess," I said.

"Is he weird or what?" she asked, diving into her lunch. "What did he want?"

"I'm not sure," I said. "He asked me if I wanted to leave school with him."

"You're kidding!" Paula exclaimed. "What a

weirdo!" She stared after him. "He'd be kind of cute if it weren't for his hair."

"Yeah," I said.

But I wasn't thinking about how cute Jack was. Or how weird his hair looked.

I was wondering if he was lying to me about not seeing Jerry Fields fall off the bleachers.

And I decided then and there, I was going to find out.

Four

The Bionic Bus always drops me off at home about four o'clock. It's a special bus that runs around the Simon College campus and the rest of town to carry handicapped people to school and work. It's pretty neat, and it gives me a lot of freedom that I wouldn't otherwise have. I can go downtown to the movies or out to the shopping center or to the public library, all without needing anyone to chauffeur me.

The hydraulic lift set me smack on the curb in front of my house and I waved goodbye to Oscar, my favorite driver.

"See you tomorrow, Chelsey," he called out and waved with his big cigar balanced between two fingers. I've never seen Oscar smoke the smelly old thing, but he always has one, unlit, in his hand.

I wheeled around to the back of the house and up the ramp my dad built to our screened-in porch. I pulled out the key dangling on a long chain around my neck and let myself into the kitchen.

My mom teaches voice in the music department at Simon College and was having to go back to school in the evenings to rehearse for a one-act opera. Even when she's not in rehearsal she doesn't have much time to cook, so I usually get dinner going. I started cooking a couple of years ago to prove to my mom that I could maneuver around the kitchen in the Blue Streak. At first she was afraid I'd burn myself on the oven door or drop something hot into my lap. But I showed her I could handle it, and now I do a lot of the cooking.

This time I started preparing a fish dinner. Just as I slid the cod into the oven, my dad emerged from his office in the basement.

"Finish your book yet?" I asked.

"No — maybe tomorrow," he said, scratching his head and yawning. "I didn't hear you come in."

"Dad, you never hear anything when you're working, especially toward the end of a book," I said.

"Really?" He looked surprised and blinked several times. His eyes were adjusting to natural light after having been under fluorescent most of the day.

"Sure," I said. "Amy and I always know that when you're close to the end of a novel we can make as much noise as we want, because you'll never hear it anyway." I paused. "Where is she, anyway?"

"Amy? Oh, she ran in a while ago and said she was

playing with a friend till dinner. Said she'd be home before five.''

Amy is my seven-year-old sister. Half the time she's a pain, and the other half we're buddies. I never know what to expect from her. I guess she's just immature.

By the time five o'clock rolled around, my fish and wild rice were done, and Amy and Mom had arrived. Mom and I made salads and we all sat down for supper.

"Did you finish your novel, Richard?" asked my mother, passing the salad dressing.

"Just a few days left, maybe by Thursday," Dad said. "Care to celebrate? Why don't we all go out for dinner when it's finished?"

"Great," Mom said. "I don't have to be at rehearsal Thursday night. The chorus is having a marathon workout. The principal singers get the night off."

"Amazing," my dad said with a smile. "Pass the rice, will you, Jenny?"

"You know that boy I saw fall from the bleachers at the game Friday night?" I piped up. "Paula said he died at the hospital."

Mom shook her head. "What a tragedy. Think what his family is going through right now."

I hadn't told them Jerry was pushed. I figured they'd just think I was letting my imagination run away with me. Or worse, they'd believe me and decide I shouldn't go to the basketball games alone anymore.

And after all, as Detective Evans had pointed out, I didn't actually *see* him pushed. I only saw the way he jerked backwards and then the dark-haired guy who looked over the rail at me.

Besides, my parents are people who tend to believe the best about people, instead of the worst. They wouldn't want to believe that a murder was committed at a Lincoln High School game, much less that I saw it happen.

"His name was Jerry Fields," I said. "He worked at Mac's, making deliveries."

"And you were the only person who saw him fall?" asked my mother.

"Uh-hunh," I nodded, finishing my last bite of wild rice.

"And you talked to the police about it?" asked my mother. "And told them everything?"

"Yes," I said.

I *had* told the police everything. They just didn't believe me when I told them Jerry was murdered.

For the next several days, I didn't see Jack, but I asked around about him. I thought maybe I'd learn something that would help me figure out why he might lie about not seeing Jerry fall. I also wanted to know why he cut off the conversation as soon as I began asking him questions about Jerry's death.

It could be that Jack was just like those people in big cities you hear about who watch someone being beaten or robbed and do nothing about it. They just don't want to get involved. Maybe Jack just didn't want to get involved.

Or maybe Jack knew more than he was saying about Jerry. And the killer.

I didn't want to think about that. Jack seemed a little strange but not evil. I was sure he didn't have anything to do with the murder.

At least, I hoped he didn't.

I didn't want the kids to think I had a crush on him or anything, so I was careful around school about how I brought up the subject of Jack Smith. I'd say, as nonchalantly as possible, "Hey, have you seen that weird kid with the green hair?" When they said "Yeah, pretty wild" or something like that, I'd say, "Who *is* he, anyway? Do you know anything *about* him?" I was careful to wrinkle up my nose a little as if I thought he was this very *strange* person.

None of the kids could tell me anything, except that he came to town about two weeks ago.

At the end of the third school day, as I slammed my locker door closed, I decided to give up. I'd learned nothing, and asking any more questions would certainly make the kids believe I was madly in love. Which, of course, I wasn't.

I wheeled down the hall and out the door to wait for the Bionic Bus. The sun was shining brightly that afternoon. All the snow from the storm had melted away, and despite a cool breeze, it felt warm next to the building.

I pulled up beside the wall to wait. The bus usually picks me up about fifteen minutes after the last bell rings, and I enjoy the wait when the weather is nice.

Out of the corner of my eye, I saw something move. I turned to see what it was.

Jack was walking toward me. But not with that cool manner I'd seen before, with his hands thrust into his pockets. This time, his jaw was set and his eyes looked deadly serious.

He stopped right in front of me.

"I hear you've been asking around about me," he said, with not a glimmer of the smiling eyes I'd seen before.

"So?" I shrugged, trying to act unruffled.

His eyes locked into mine, but not like a snake charmer this time. More like a snake.

"Chelsey," he said, "you don't want to know about me."

"Why not?" I asked.

"Because I'm trouble." His eyes never left mine.

"So who's going to help me figure out what happened to Jerry Fields?" I asked, staring right back.

There was that stiffening again when I mentioned the dead boy.

"That's why I'm telling you to stay away from

me," he said. "You're good. You probably always do the right thing. Most people aren't like you, you know."

"But —"

"And forget about Jerry's death," he said, lowering his voice, but hissing through his teeth. "You don't know what you're getting into."

"What *am* I getting into?" I asked.

"Just stay away!" he said angrily. "Just stay away, or you'll get yourself in deep trouble, I can promise you that!"

And with that, he turned abruptly and strode off around the side of the school.

Five

Now there was no doubt in my mind. Jack knew a lot more about Jerry's death than he was admitting.

But the jackpot question was this: Did he just *know* about it, or was he actually *involved*? I was beginning to wonder. Why else would he tell me to forget about Jerry's death? Who was he protecting? A *murderer*?

Dad met me at the back door when I arrived home. He held up a two-inch thick manuscript. "Here it is," he said proudly. "Finished."

"Great!" I exclaimed. "When do I get to read it?"

"Just as soon as I get it copied," Dad said. "You'll be my first reader. Your mom is too busy these days."

"Did the butler do it?" I asked, teasing. Dad's

books are usually mysteries, and the butler's never been the murderer yet.

"Wait and see," Dad said, his eyes gleaming.

"So do we get to go out tonight to celebrate?" I asked.

"Yes," Dad said. "As soon as your mother gets home. She called and said she'd be home soon."

"Where are we going?" I asked.

"What's your stomach in the mood for?" Dad asked back.

"But *you* wrote the book!" I said. "You choose!"

"Honey, I'm so glad the book is finished before my editor's deadline, I probably won't even taste the food. You and Amy decide."

Suddenly I had a thought. "Say, how about Mac's Pizza? We haven't been there in a while."

"Fine," Dad agreed, "as long as we go early enough that we beat the high school mob. I'm not crazy about sitting around with two hundred sixteen-year-olds."

"Okay," I said.

I wheeled through our kitchen and into the living room and down the hall to my bedroom. One reason my parents bought this older Tudor house seven years ago was because of the hardwood floors. Except for the kitchen and bathroom, the whole house has varnished oak floorboards, so it's very easy for me to get around, and I can really zoom down the hallway if no one gets in my way. My parents talk about the "aesthetic quality" of hardwood floors as opposed to carpeting, and I know my mom likes the way the music room rings when she sings and plays the piano, but the real reason we bought the house was because of my wheelchair. My parents are always worried about how I'll get around, so they were especially pleased to get this particular house.

My bedroom is on the ground floor, of course. In fact, most of the house is on the main floor, with just Amy's room and a storage room upstairs. Actually, it isn't really a second floor, it's more like a dormer. And I can go up there anytime I want to. We have an electric lift that carries a seat like an elevator along the stairs, and I can go up and down with no problem. I can get to the basement in the same way.

My room is my favorite spot in the house, I guess, because it is truly my own. I picked out the furniture myself, mostly at auctions and antique stores. All of it is oak and was probably made when my grandparents were growing up. Mom helped me refinish the dressing table two years ago. I love to sit in front of it and brush my hair. It makes me feel very glamorous.

The walls are covered with posters of all my favorite movie and rock stars. Sometimes when I'm feeling down, I lie on my bed and have conversations with these people. Of course, I don't ever tell anyone I do this. They'd think I was nuts.

Today, though, I didn't talk to any of my movie star friends. I turned on my radio and lay on my bed and thought about Jack.

He sure was a strange guy. There was just something about him that was different from all the other boys I knew. The way he carried himself, for one thing. Not all slumped over the way most boys are, as if they think everyone's looking at them, and they want to crawl into a hole and hide.

Jack looked so *cool*, so comfortable, as if he'd already lived a whole lifetime before he turned fourteen.

The only time he wasn't cool was when I talked about Jerry. *"Just stay away, or you'll get yourself in deep trouble,"* he'd said. He had to know who killed Jerry, or he wouldn't have said that.

I heard Mom and then Amy come through the back door, so I thought I'd better get ready to go to Mac's. I wanted to go there, partly just to see again where Jerry'd worked, and I thought maybe just being there, where Jerry had spent so much time, I might think of something that would help me figure out what to do about what I saw at the game.

We arrived at Mac's about five-thirty, and the place was already beginning to fill up.

As soon as we'd pushed through the heavy glass door, I pointed out a booth in the back and suggested we sit there, out of the way. I knew Dad would agree to that.

I slipped into the booth, choosing a spot where I could see the whole room.

Mac, the owner, was talking to some kids. Then he disappeared into the back office.

"Hi, I'm Wendy, and I'll be your server tonight." The waitress looked about sixteen, I guess, and wore an orange and brown uniform with *Mac's* stitched on the front pocket.

We ordered a large taco pizza, and Wendy left.

"Dad, can I play the jukebox?" Amy asked.

"Both you girls may choose one record," Dad said and fished two quarters out of his pocket.

Amy jumped up and scampered across the room to the jukebox, and moments later, the room was vibrating with rock 'n' roll. I'd told her to play anything other than a romantic ballad with my quarter. I just wasn't in that kind of mood.

Before Amy got back, Wendy came with our drinks.

"Say, did you know Jerry Fields, the boy who died at the basketball game?" I asked her.

"Sure," she said. "Too bad. He was a nice kid."

"That's what I heard," I said. "Did everyone like him?"

She shrugged. "I dunno. I s'pose."

"What hours did he work?" I asked. I noticed my mom and dad look at each other curiously.

"Uhm. I think he worked the six to ten shift. No, maybe that's wrong. I saw him here sometimes in the late afternoon. Oh, I don't know. I'll ask the manager. Here're your drinks."

"Oh, don't bother asking," I said. "It's not a big deal. I was just wondering." Wendy left.

"Why did you want to know his work hours?" my mother asked, tucking a strand of her blond hair behind one ear.

"Just curious," I said.

I hoped Wendy didn't decide to ask the manager about Jerry's hours. If I were going to investigate, I'd better do it with a low profile. After all, Jack had said big trouble would be in store for me if I continued asking questions.

Within fifteen minutes, our pizza was steaming in front of us.

"Dig in, guys!" Dad said.

"No, wait. First," Mom said, holding up her Coke glass, "I'd like to propose a toast. To your latest book, Richard," she said, smiling at Dad. "May it become a best seller."

"Ha. Fat chance," Dad said, grinning. But I could tell he was really pleased.

"To the book!" Amy and I said. Then we dug in.

"It's impossible to eat one of these and still look cool," I said, looking at the glob of cheese that had fallen onto my plate. My family laughed.

Just then the glass door opened from the street, and I nearly choked. Jack Smith came in hurriedly and, without any hesitation, walked to the manager's office door and rapped three times. The door was abruptly yanked open, and there in the doorway I saw a face with dark curly hair and piercing black eyes.

It was the guy from the bleachers! The guy who'd pushed Jerry Fields to his death! What was Jack doing here — with the murderer?

Jack disappeared with him inside the office.

"Chelsey, what's wrong? You look as if you've seen a ghost!" my mother said.

My heart was beating hard and my palms were sweating. But I couldn't tell them what was going on. I couldn't explain it all, especially not here and now.

"Oh, nothing," I said, trying to sound casual. "I just thought I saw a girl from my school wearing the same blouse I bought last weekend." I managed a smile. "I was wrong. It's completely different."

"Oh, these girls and their clothes." Dad sighed and sipped his Coke.

What was Jack doing here with the guy who murdered Jerry? My heart felt crushed. Not because Jack was all that special to me, but just because I didn't think he was the sort of person who could get mixed up with murderers.

But if he knew the dark-haired guy, he could've known all about the murder. Maybe he knew it was going to happen. Maybe he even helped plan it.

For the first time ever, the taco pizza tasted terrible.

"Don't you want your pizza?" Mom asked me.

"No, I guess not," I said. "I'm not as hungry as I thought."

Mom and Dad watched me with concern in their eyes but didn't say anything. Amy ate merrily along, as if she didn't notice that the mood had changed at our table.

Just then, Wendy stopped in front of us. "Oh, say, I was curious about Jerry's hours, too, so I just asked Ron, the manager. He said Jerry worked the six to ten shift. Just like I thought."

"Oh. Thanks," I said, shrugging as if it didn't make any difference to me.

She'd asked about Jerry. She asked the murderer about his victim, probably saying one of the customers wants to know!

I looked up, and there, next to the manager's office, watching Wendy at our table, was Ron, the murderer! Wendy hurried away to take someone else's order. Now the dark-haired man's gaze fell on *me*. Just like at the basketball game. And there was no doubt in my mind that he recognized who I was, and knew I was the one who'd asked Wendy about Jerry.

The manager's door pushed open and Jack stepped out, speaking to Ron. Jack stopped, seeing that the man was distracted, and followed his gaze to me.

A look of horror passed over his face, and he turned suddenly and vanished into the office again.

41

My dad stood up and held my mom's jacket for her and then helped me maneuver out of the booth and into my chair.

The cash register is located at the front of the place, near the door. My family weaved around tables through the crowd to the door. Dad took out his checkbook and began to write.

"Your server is busy now, so I'll be glad to help you." Ron had slipped in front of Wendy and was watching my dad make out his check.

Ron didn't look at me while my dad wrote. He just stood there and smiled a little at my mother.

"Thank you very much, sir," Ron said and nodded to Dad. He took the check and nodded again as we turned toward the door.

I glanced back over my shoulder. Ron was studying the check.

Our address and phone number! They were printed on the check!

Ron now knew who I was and where I lived!

My dad opened the big glass door and a stiff breeze pressed into our faces. My heart pounding, I glanced one more time over my shoulder.

Ron stood there, his eyes dark with anger, boring holes right through me.

Six

"Hey, Che-e-elsey! Someone's here to see you!"

Amy scampered into my room and landed on my bed with a thump.

"Who is it?" I asked, my heart skipping a beat. Could it be Ron from Mac's Pizza? Would he dare walk up to the front door and ask for me?

"Paula," Amy said, taking a bite out of the apple she was holding.

"Oh," I said, relieved. "Tell her to come on in. How can you eat after all that pizza?"

Amy got up off the bed and skipped out of the room. "Daddy says I have a hollow leg," she called back over her shoulder.

I'd been sitting at my desk trying to concentrate on my English homework ever since we'd come back from Mac's. But let me tell you, trying to concentrate on prepositional phrases while someone is probably plotting a fatal "accident" for you is practically impossible.

If Ron murdered Jerry, and I was sure that he *did*, and he knew that I saw it all happen, wouldn't it make sense that he'd want to get rid of *me*, too?

I was really scared.

"Hi, Chelsey," Paula said, stopping in the doorway.

"Hi," I said. "What's up?"

"Well, I had to go to the orthodontist this morning, and I missed Erwin's science class. So I thought I'd drop by and get the assignment."

"Oh, we read a couple of pages in the text and then answered questions at the end of the section. It was pretty easy."

"For you," Paula said, rolling her eyes upward.

"For you, too," I said.

I do pretty well in school, but I'm no brain. And Paula gets very good grades when she wants to.

Paula grinned and plopped down on my bed.

"The assignment was the excuse I used to get over here. The real reason is because I heard something today that will really blow your mind. I had to come over and tell you!"

"What?" I asked. Most of the gossip around school usually runs through Paula at some point. I have to admit, while I don't always spread what I hear, I really enjoy listening to the stories going around about the kids at school.

Paula licked her lips and leaned toward me.

"Remember the other day at lunch when you talked to that green-haired Smith kid?" My heart skipped a beat, and I nodded. "I *told* you that day he was weird. Just wait till I tell you what I heard about him."

"What?" I said.

"Well, my cousin lives in River Falls and went to school with him. That's where Smith comes from. I talked to her on the phone tonight, and I just happened to mention we have this green-haired kid at school, and we realized he's the same one!"

"Yes?"

"Smith was always in trouble at school and even with the police," Paula said, lowering her voice and narrowing her eyes.

"What do you mean?"

"Well, the biggest thing was a charge of assault with a deadly weapon. He was in a fight and nearly killed a kid with a knife. And any time something was missing, he was always the chief suspect. I don't know if they ever pinned theft on him or not, but everyone *knew* he'd stolen stuff. He was suspended all the time for skipping school. And he asked *you* to skip school with him right in the middle of the day!"

"Oh," I said, "yes."

"He comes from a really bad home."

"Bad in what way?" I asked.

"Well, he doesn't have a father for one thing."

"I know some kids who don't have fathers living with them, but their homes aren't bad at all," I pointed out.

"Yeah, but Jack's never *had* a father. His mother never got married. And she's a drunk," Paula said, looking as if she'd proved her point.

"Oh," I said, feeling rotten.

"Smith and his mom probably moved here after he got into so much trouble in their other town." Paula flopped down on the bed on her stomach and propped herself up on her elbows. "I told you he was weird. I just knew we'd hear something like this about him."

"Yeah," I said. And Paula didn't know the half of it.

"Well, you'd better stay away from him. He could be dangerous," Paula said. "I saw Debbie Barton on the way over here, and I told her about Jack Smith, so you *know* it'll be all over school by tomorrow. All the kids'll be talking about him. I bet he'll wish he hadn't moved here!"

"Yeah," I said. "I wouldn't want to be in his place."

"You wouldn't *be* in his place," Paula said, getting up from the bed. "Well, I guess I'd better get home. I told Mom I'd just be a few minutes."

"Okay," I said. "Well, thanks for coming over, Paula."

"Well, I couldn't let the juiciest gossip of the

whole school year go by without telling you about it," Paula said. "See you at school tomorrow. And if you see Jack Smith, you'd better head in the opposite direction."

"Okay," I said.

After she left, I transferred myself to my bed, picked up my guitar and absentmindedly strummed a few chords.

My guitar lesson was the next day but I just couldn't concentrate on the music. Normally, my music cheers me up, but that night it didn't work.

I was scared and sad, both at the same time. Scared because the guy at Mac's knew who I was and sad because of what Paula had just told me about Jack. If Jack could cut up a kid in a knife fight, he could be involved in Jerry's murder. And I'd just seen him with the murderer. But in spite of everything I'd heard about Jack, I still liked him in a way. I don't know why. It was very confusing.

Suddenly, I was startled by the ringing of the telephone on my nightstand. I laid my guitar on the bed and grabbed up the receiver.

"Hello?" I said.

There was silence on the line.

"Hello?" I said again.

Again, silence.

I was about to hang up, when he finally spoke. A low, whispery kind of voice.

"I know where you live," he said.

"What?" I said, knowing who it must be.

"I know where you live," the voice repeated. "And if you don't start minding your own business, I'll have to set up a little accident for *you*."

"Who is this?" I stammered, feeling my heart hammering into my ribs.

"You don't know what you're getting into," the husky voice said, and the line went dead.

I hung up the telephone, my hand shaking uncontrollably.

I lay on the bed trembling and played and replayed the telephone conversation over in my mind.

Of course, that call must have come from Ron, the manager at Mac's, the man who pushed Jerry Fields off the bleachers at the game. He had just found out where I live by the address on my dad's check. And he knew the phone number. He saw me at the game and the waitress had told him I was asking questions about Jerry's work schedule. The call *should* have come from Ron.

But it didn't.

I had recognized the voice, even though it was low and whispery. And he said just what he'd said to me once before, "You don't know what you're getting into."

It was Jack.

And he said he was planning an accident for *me*.

Seven

I don't like to play games with people. By that, I mean I'd rather be direct and say what I want to say, instead of beating around the bush.

And if someone wants me to know something, I expect them to come out and say it right to my face.

I'd never gotten an anonymous phone call before. I think people who make anonymous calls are creeps. Cowardly creeps because they aren't willing to show their faces and say what they have to say.

Obviously, Jack was a cowardly creep, and then a whole lot more. But I intended to deal with him directly, not over the phone like some jerk coward.

Maybe I should've been afraid of him. After all, he was involved in one murder and threatened me with another. But at least right then, I was just angry. And I mean really angry.

As soon as I got to school the next morning, I

started looking for him, my heart beating hard, my jaw feeling tight, and my hands clenching the arms of the wheelchair till my knuckles turned white.

Once I caught sight of him down at the end of the hall, but when I got there, he was gone. I don't know if he was avoiding me or was just hard to find that day.

Then just before fourth hour, I saw him at his locker, spinning his combination lock. I wheeled right up to him.

"Jack Smith," I said boldly.

He turned to look at me. I don't think it was my imagination; he looked surprised.

"Yeah?" he said, swinging open his locker and slapping his math book in on the top shelf. He pretended to be thinking about something else, but I could see him watching me out of the corner of his eye. What a difference from the first few times I had seen him. Some snake charmer!

"I want to talk to you," I said.

"Yeah?" he said again, turning toward me and leaning against the locker, some of his cool returning. "So, what's up?"

Jennifer Wilcox was standing at her locker right next to him. She was lingering over her social studies book as if she were studying it hard. I knew better. Jennifer couldn't care less about social studies. She was eavesdropping.

"Not here and not now," I said, lowering my voice. "I want to talk to you right after school. I'll meet you where I talked to you the other day, at the bus stop."

"I'm going to be busy," Jack said, now looking right into my eyes.

"Maybe you'd rather I go to the police?" I asked pointedly, but with my voice still soft.

He flinched, so I knew I'd scared him at least a little.

"Like I said, I'll meet you right after school. Don't make me wait." And with that, I whipped my chair around and whisked back down the hall, smiling a little in triumph because I'd surprised him with a threat of my own.

I hardly heard a word in class the rest of that day, I was thinking so much about my meeting with Jack after school. I saw him across the lunchroom at noon, but he didn't even look my way.

He was alone, as usual. The kids were talking about him, just as Paula had said they would, spreading around the story of his home life and all the trouble he'd been in before he came here. I wondered if he knew they were talking about him. I guessed he did.

When the bell ending the school day rang I headed for my locker in a hurry, got what I needed for homework, and headed out the door.

I pulled my chair into my usual spot next to the school building and waited.

I watched all the kids run out of the building and grab bikes, hop into cars, or climb onto school buses and head for home.

And no Jack.

The kids out for track came jogging by and some of them waved to me, and several others played catch with a baseball and gloves, and the time dragged on.

And no Jack.

So he isn't coming, I thought, my heart sinking. *Now what should I do? Go to the police? Tell them I know who murdered Jerry Fields?* They still thought his fall was an accident, as far as I knew.

And I still had no proof.

Just then, I looked up to see Jack strolling along the side of the building, his hands in his pockets, cool as could be. He walked right up to me and leaned against the building, his hands still tucked in his jeans.

"So what's up?" he asked with a little shrug, as if he had absolutely no idea what I was going to say.

I admit I was thrown off a little, thinking he wasn't going to show up. The anger that had given me so much confidence earlier and had come to a sharp focus at the end of the school day had somehow melted away when he didn't appear right after school. My timing was thrown off, because I didn't have the edge that nervous energy gives me.

"You know what's up, Jack," I said, struggling to regain my composure.

He sighed. "Chelsey, you want to tell me what's going on?"

"You called me last night," I said. "Anonymously."

I had to give him credit. He didn't bat an eyelash. "*I* called you?" He shook his head. "Why would I call you? I told you to stay away from me."

I looked at him directly in the eyes. "I recognized your voice, Jack. Nice try."

He paused only slightly. "You're wrong, Chelsey. But if someone *did* call you, doesn't that tell you something?"

"Like what?" I said, challenging him.

"Look, I don't know about this phone call of yours, but if I were you, I'd be careful about going around asking questions about people you know nothing about."

"You mean, like Jerry Fields?" I asked.

"Like anybody, especially Jerry Fields."

"And what if I don't?" I asked him. "What are you going to do? Kill me?"

Jack flinched. "Why would I do something like that?"

"Isn't that what you said you'd do? On the phone last night? Didn't you say you'd have to plan a little accident for me, too? Just like the accident Jerry Fields had!"

"Look, Chelsey —"

"No, *you* look, Jack," I said, my voice getting stronger, along with my confidence. "I'm not in the habit of being threatened, not over the phone or in person. Threatening to end a person's life is against the law, in case you aren't aware of it, but I guess you don't much care about breaking the law, anyway. I'd say murder is against the law, and you went along with Jerry Fields's murder, and now you're trying to cover it up by scaring me into shutting up about it. But don't threaten me, Jack Smith, because I'm not afraid of you! Not one little bit!" I stopped right there and glared angrily at him.

He stood straight up in front of me looking dazed. "What?" he said. "I went along with Jerry's murder? Is that what you think?"

"You were there at the basketball game," I said. "You know the guy who pushed him off the bleachers. I saw you with him last night at Mac's. Then you threatened my life if I didn't stop investigating the murder. Are you afraid I'll tell the police you were part of the plan?"

He stared at me, shocked.

"Chelsey," he said. "You've got it all wrong. I didn't have anything to do with Jerry's murder."

"How stupid do you think I am?" I cried. "And now you'll try and kill me, too, if I don't shut up."

Jack collapsed against the building and put his head in his hands. "No, Chelsey, you're wrong.

You're wrong." He paused a moment as the Bionic Bus approached.

"I've got to go, Jack, or I'm going to miss the bus,"

"No, Chelsey, don't go now. Isn't there another bus later?" He asked me urgently, almost begging.

"Not for forty minutes," I said. "I've got to get home."

"Chelsey, wait, will you?" he asked. "I need to talk to you about this. I need to explain."

"I can't," I said.

"Chelsey —"

I gazed up at him, at his crazy green hair, at his clear blue eyes pleading with me to stay and clear up this mess.

I sighed. "Okay," I said, shaking my head, and I waved to Oscar on the bus.

The door swung open. "Not riding today, Chelsey?" he yelled to me.

"I'll take the next one, thanks, Oscar," I yelled back.

"Okay," he called and waved.

The door closed and the bus slowly moved off on its route.

Jack turned back to me. "Thanks, Chelsey." He paused. "I didn't have any idea that you thought *I* was involved in Jerry's death."

"So what did you want me to believe, Jack?" I asked.

"The truth," Jack said. "Come on, let's go somewhere private."

"Like where?" I asked, thinking for an instant that if he *did* want to kill me, he'd take me somewhere private.

But I didn't really believe Jack was a bad person. He couldn't be.

But then, how could he have knifed a kid in a fight? I just didn't know. But I wanted so badly to trust him.

"How about the football field?" he suggested. "No one is usually down there this time of the day."

I nodded and he pivoted my wheelchair around, and we started off, him pushing me along the sidewalk and then the dirt path to the field.

He wheeled me over to the bottom row of bleachers. Then he climbed onto the second-row bench and squinted into the sun.

"My favorite time of year," he said then. He made a fist with one hand and slapped it softly into his other palm, gazing off toward the hills surrounding the town.

"It's hard to believe we had a snowstorm just last week," I said. That made me remember the night it snowed so hard, the night Jerry was murdered.

I knew by the look on his face, Jack was thinking the same thing.

"Okay, let me start at the beginning," Jack said.

Then he shook his head and mumbled softly, "I never thought I'd be telling you this."

"Go ahead," I said. "I have to know what happened. Everything."

"Okay, well, I moved here almost three weeks ago." I nodded, and he continued. "I needed some spending money, so I thought I'd get a job after school. I found one cleaning up after hours at Mac's Pizza."

"So that's why you were there," I said.

"Yeah. I'm usually there when the place is closed, but last night I went in to pick up my paycheck." He shook his head again. "Man, I was really surprised to see you there."

"Not half as surprised as *I* was," I said.

"Anyway," he continued, staring down between his feet, "the afternoon of the big snowstorm, I'd gone right from school to Mac's. Mac was there, but soon after I started cleaning the floor, he left to run an errand. I thought Mac seemed like a nice guy, he was always real friendly around me. But then, I hadn't known him very long."

"But Mac isn't the guy I saw last night, right? The guy you were talking to when you picked up your check?" I asked.

"No. You saw Ron Whitehill, the manager. Ron's maybe nineteen or twenty. Mac, the owner, is an older guy, probably in his forties."

"Okay," I said.

"So I was washing the floor, right?" Jack said. I could tell he was feeling a little nervous about what he was going to tell me. "Well, the phone rings, and nobody's there but me. So I figure I'd better answer it, maybe take a message for Mac.

"Well, I'd heard Mac answer the phone a lot of times, and he always'd pick up the phone and say, 'Yeah?' in this hurried kind of voice. Just like that, 'Yeah?' So, I grabbed the phone and just like Mac, I said, 'Yeah?' into the phone without identifying myself or anything."

I nodded so he'd know I was following his story.

"Well, whoever was calling thought I was Mac. And he said one thing. And then he hung up."

"What did he say?" I asked.

Jack ran a hand over the top of his head and blew out a breath of air. "He said, 'Tonight's the night. Fields's going to the game.' Then he hung up."

"He was talking about the murder!" I said softly.

"I didn't know what was going on," Jack said. "But it sounded really fishy."

"Was Ron the person on the telephone?"

"Yeah," Jack said. "I recognized his voice. I knew Jerry Fields a little and he seemed like a nice enough guy. So I decided to go to the game and watch Jerry from a distance to try to figure out what was going on. I never thought Jerry'd be *killed*."

"So I *did* see you duck under the bleachers just before Jerry fell!" I said.

"Yeah, I saw you coming," Jack said. "I'd been trying to find Jerry, but I lost him in the crowd. I wanted to cross to the other side of the gym without being seen, so I circled around behind the bleachers. That was just before Ron pushed Jerry off the top row. The whole crowd was so busy watching the players on the court that no one even saw or paid attention to Jerry sitting behind the pep band. And no one saw Ron push him. It probably took all of two seconds. A murder, in a gymnasium full of people."

"And you listened to me talk to that policeman, Detective Evans," I said.

"Right. I wondered what you'd seen. I was hoping you'd tell the cop you saw Ron push Jerry."

"Why did you come over and talk to me?" I asked. "And why didn't you tell me all of this then?"

"I thought you'd be in a lot of danger if you knew anything," he said. "I didn't want to tell you any of this. That's why I told you to stay clear of me and Jerry's accident."

"But *you* didn't have anything to do with it!" I said.

"Listen," he said. "You know the saying 'innocent until proven guilty'?"

I nodded.

"Well, the real world isn't like that. You're guilty until proven innocent. Believe me, I know," he said. Then he added in a soft voice, staring at his feet, "That's the way the world is. It's a snake pit."

I thought about the stories going around about him, and I wondered if he was thinking about those things.

"I can't really believe that," I said.

"You live in a different world than I do," he said and shrugged. "Anyway, that's why I called you last night. I'd already told you to mind your own business and that didn't stop you. You kept asking questions, and then I saw you at Mac's. Wendy came into the office when I was there and asked about Jerry's work schedule. She said a customer was asking. Ron answered her question and then followed her into the dining area and watched her walk right over to you. Then I knew you were in real danger. Ron took your dad's check, you know."

"Yeah, I saw him studying the name," I said.

"And the address," Jack said. "I didn't know how else to warn you to be careful. So I called your nouse, pretending to be Ron. I thought I'd scare you." He smiled a little. "You don't scare so easy."

"If I hadn't recognized your voice, I'd have been plenty scared," I said. He didn't say anything, but his eyes hung on mine for a moment. I glanced away first. "Jack, why would Ron and Mac want to kill Jerry Fields? Everyone says he was a nice guy."

"I've been working on that," Jack said, rubbing his palms together and leaning toward me with his elbows on his knees. "Something's going on at Mac's. Mac and Ron get phone calls that don't sound like pizza orders. I only hear their half of the conversation while I'm working, and they don't say much. But twice, I saw Mac unlock his desk drawer and take out a little black notebook right after one of those calls. He looked at it, and then over at me to see if I was watching him. Then he shut the book real quick and locked it back up in the drawer."

"What do you think is going on?" I asked.

"Well, it's just a guess, but I'm beginning to think Mac's is delivering something else along with pizza," he said.

"You mean like drugs?" I asked, astonished.

"Maybe," Jack said. "I just don't know. But it's something big enough and dangerous enough that Jerry Fields was killed because he found out about it."

I let out a big breath.

There was a long pause.

"So what'll we do now?" I asked.

Jack said nothing.

"Go to the police?" I asked.

Still, he was quiet.

"Jack, I think we'd better go and talk to that policeman, Detective Evans." I watched Jack for a moment. He sat on the bleacher, staring off into space. "Jack, we have to go to the police."

"I knew you'd say that," he finally said, very quietly.

"Well, why not? I'd say we're both in danger at this point," I said. "If Mac and Ron find out that we know —"

"I don't know," Jack said, shaking his head.

"What's the matter?" I asked. "What's wrong with talking to the police?"

Again, the strange silence.

"Jack, you *aren't* involved in this, are you?" I asked.

He looked up sharply. "Of course not!" he said. His cheeks turned red. "I just don't like cops much," he said, and he turned his head away. "They aren't my favorite people, let's put it that way."

"We're just going to tell Detective Evans what we know," I said.

"And what if he accuses me of helping to pull it off?" Jack asked. "Don't you think he might wonder how I figured out the drug part of all this?"

"But you're innocent," I said.

"Chelsey." Jack paused and clenched his fists. "If I turn in a report like this, they're going to investigate *me*, too."

"So?" I asked, stupidly.

"So I have a *record*," he said softly.

I didn't say anything.

"A *police* record."

At last, I understood. Boy, was I dumb. Of course,

that's why he'd kept quiet! He didn't want his past life from River Falls following him here.

"Chelsey," he said, "I should tell you something before —"

"Jack, it's okay," I said. "I already know you were in trouble with the police in River Falls."

"So you heard?" he said. "I figured you'd hear the gossip. I know what they're saying about me."

"Jack," I said, "I heard, but it's okay —"

"No, it's *not* okay!" Jack said, raising his voice in anger. "It's okay for you, because you're not the one they're gossiping about. It's me! And they don't have any idea what they're talking about! What'd they say I was accused of?"

I didn't say anything for a moment.

"Did they say that I was accused of knifing a kid?"

I nodded.

"Well, what they don't know, and what the police refused to believe, was that the kid came after *me* with a knife. And in fighting him off, I managed to get the knife away from him, but he was cut in the scuffle."

He paused.

"And did they say that I'm a thief?"

Again, I nodded.

"Did they bother to tell you that no evidence was ever found to prove that I ever broke into any of the places they said I did?"

"No, I guess not," I said.

"And did you believe it, Chelsey?" Jack asked. "Did you think I really did those things?"

"I didn't know, Jack," I said meekly. "Why did they accuse you?"

"Because of who I am and where I come from," he said angrily.

There was a long pause.

"Damn," he said softly. "I thought it might be different here."

"Would it make any difference if I said that I don't think you were guilty of doing anything wrong?" I asked.

Jack looked at the ground. Then he said softly, "Well, you'd be wrong there, too."

He didn't explain what he meant by that, and I guessed it really wasn't any of my business. Then he sighed.

"Well, I guess we don't have much choice, do we? I mean, about going to the cops."

"I guess not," I said. "When do you want to go?"

"Come on," he said, jumping off the bleachers and grabbing the handles to my chair. "Let's get this over with."

Eight

I called my dad to tell him I'd be late getting home. I told him I was going downtown on the bus. Of course, he probably thought that meant I was going shopping. But I didn't tell him that. The police station happens to be right on the edge of the business district.

We didn't have to wait more than ten minutes for the Bionic Bus to arrive. Usually, nonhandicapped people don't ride on it, but no one says anything if a handicapped person brings a friend along. Paula's ridden with me quite a few times.

We rode along in silence for a while. I could tell Jack was nervous about talking to Detective Evans. He kept his hands clenched into fists and seemed very distracted, looking out of the window most of the way.

"Jack?" I said, finally, when we were about half-

65

way there. "Are you okay?" He jumped a little when I said his name, and he looked at me.

"Sure," he said.

"It'll be okay, Jack," I said. "Detective Evans seems like a really nice man."

"Yeah," Jack said, still looking out the window.

"Have you had bad experiences with cops?" I asked.

"Yeah," Jack said again, but didn't offer any explanation.

The Bionic Bus stopped right in front of the police station, and Jack rode the lift with me down to the cement. I turned to him and asked, "Ready?"

He nodded and pushed my chair to the front door of the station.

Right inside, a uniformed officer sat at a desk on a high platform. He looked up when we approached and eyed us curiously. First, me in my wheelchair, then Jack, with his green hair.

"Can I help you?" he asked in a friendly tone.

I spoke, thinking Jack would want to be quiet. "We're here to see Detective Evans," I said. "Is he available?"

"Take a left turn down the hall. His office is the second on the right," the man said to me. He glanced back at Jack and nodded goodbye.

We followed the route through the building and came to a stop in front of an office with "Evans" painted on the glass door, which stood slightly ajar.

A long moment passed. I looked up at Jack.

"Why don't you tap on the door?" I suggested.

Jack hesitated a second, then leaned over my chair to knock lightly.

"Come in," a deep voice said from inside the office.

Jack swung the door open and pushed me inside. Detective Evans sat behind his desk. His uniform jacket was draped over a chair at the side of the room, and he appeared to be working on some papers.

"Well, hello," he said, looking surprised to see us. "Come on in and make yourselves comfortable."

He stood up and pulled a chair sitting in front of his desk out of the way to make room for me. Then he nodded to the chair and said to Jack, "Have a seat."

Jack sat down without a word.

"Didn't I speak with you out at the high school?" Detective Evans asked me. "After Jerry Fields's accident?"

"Yes," I said. "Remember, I saw Jerry fall."

"Yes," he said and nodded. "Chelsey, right?"

"Right," I said. "Chelsey Bernard. And this is Jack Smith."

"How are you, Jack?" he said, leaning over the desk to shake Jack's hand. "Is this about the accident?"

"Yes," I said.

"Do you have any information that could help us?" the detective asked.

"Remember when I told you that Jerry was pushed off the bleachers?" I asked.

"I certainly do," he said.

"Well," I said and glanced at Jack, "we have something to tell you that might convince you that Jerry was murdered."

Detective Evans leaned forward with his elbows on his desk. "Okay," he said. "What have you got?"

I looked at Jack. He was watching the detective, kind of sizing him up. I couldn't tell by the look on his face what he was thinking.

"Jack," I said, "do you want to tell this part?"

Jack glanced over at me and moved uneasily in his chair. Detective Evans's gaze shifted over to Jack.

"Anything that could help us on this case, we'd really appreciate, Jack," Evans said.

Jack nodded and cleared his throat nervously. "Okay," he said. "Well, I work at Mac's Pizza after hours, cleaning up the floor mostly."

Then he went on and told Detective Evans about answering the phone and hearing Ron's voice say, "Tonight's the night. Fields's going to the game."

He described how he followed Jerry from a distance in the gym until he lost him in the crowd, and then ducked under the bleachers when he saw me coming.

Detective Evans listened closely to Jack and nodded encouragement while Jack told the story.

"I don't know why anyone would want to kill Jerry Fields," Jack said. "Unless Jerry knew about something he wasn't supposed to know."

"What do you think that was?" the detective asked.

"I'm not sure, but I s'pose it could be — drugs."

"Why drugs?" Evans asked.

Then Jack told him about the strange phone calls Mac had taken and about the little black notebook that his boss seemed so secretive about.

Detective Evans rested his chin on his hand and stared into space thoughtfully.

"Sounds like something's going on, all right," he said. "Matter of fact, we've suspected something like this for several months, but never had anything to go on."

"Really?" Jack asked. He looked at me and I smiled.

"Detective Evans," I said, "Ron knows who I am and where I live." I told him about having pizza with my family.

"Hmmm." He nodded thoughtfully. After a moment he said, "Here's what I want you two to do. Jack, don't go back to work at Mac's, at least until we have a chance to investigate what you've just told me."

Jack started to protest but Evans held up a hand. "It may be dangerous for you, Jack. If Ron mentions to Mac that he called just before the murder, they'll know who answered the phone. Obviously, up to this point, they haven't talked about it."

Evans looked at me. "And you, young lady, could be in a lot of danger. So stay away from Mac's. And, at least for a while, don't go out alone, okay?" I nodded. "Do your parents know about all of this?"

"No," I said. "No need to worry them. I'll be careful."

"You'd better have a chat with them when you get home," he said. "Have them call me if they want to." He turned to Jack. "What about your parents?"

Jack shook his head and looked at the floor. "No," he said, "my mom doesn't know."

"Same advice for you, then," Evans said. "It'd be best if they were all aware of the situation. They'll make sure you kids don't go out alone. I don't think Ron and Mac would try anything in broad daylight while you're in the company of other people."

"You mean, like at a basketball game?" Jack said, with a little smile.

"Well, you see, Jerry was different," Detective Evans said. "Jerry didn't know they might come after him. If he did, he could've yelled and attracted attention. They may know that you know about them. They're probably sure Chelsey knows. They wouldn't come after you in public. But just be careful."

We thanked him as we got up, and he shook our

hands. "Thanks to both of you for coming in," he said. "We'll be in touch."

Out on the sidewalk, Jack pushed me along in silence for a while. Finally I said, "So, are you going to quit your job, Jack? Seems like a good idea."

"I don't know," Jack said.

We rode along a little bit farther.

"What did you think about what Detective Evans said?" I asked.

"What do you mean?" Jack asked.

"He said they'd suspected Mac's of drug dealing before," I said. "Weren't you surprised?"

"Yeah," was all he said.

"Jack, what are you thinking about?" I asked.

"Hmmm?" he said absentmindedly. "Oh, nothing."

He waited for the Bionic Bus with me, but when we saw it a block away he suddenly turned to me and said, "Well, I'll see you at school tomorrow, Chelsey."

"Aren't you going to ride on the bus?" I asked.

"No, I think I'll walk home," he said. "I have a lot to think about."

"Just promise me you'll stay away from Mac's, okay?" I said.

"Yeah, I promise. I won't go over there."

"And if you decide to, you'll call me first, right?" I said.

"Chelsey, I'm not going to Mac's, I promise," he

said. Then he smiled at me a little. "Don't worry about me, Chelsey."

"Hey, I'm not worried about you," I said, feeling my cheeks getting hot, "I just don't want to miss anything exciting."

"There won't be anything exciting," he said. "Not yet, anyway."

Just then the bus stopped in front of me and the big doors yawned open.

"What do you mean, 'not yet'?" I asked.

"Bye, Chelsey," he said. He turned and started off.

"What do you mean, 'not yet'?" I yelled after him.

But he continued walking away from me with his hands stuffed into his pockets.

Nine

My guitar lesson is right after supper at my teacher's house. Mr. Edberg is a great guitar player and an excellent teacher. He plays in jazz bands and teaches part-time at the college.

Usually my lessons are fun, because I practice a lot. Usually.

This time was different, though. I'd been so distracted with the murder and suspecting Jack and all that I'd hardly picked up my guitar all week.

"You're not quite with it today, Chelsey," Mr. Edberg said after about ten minutes. "Just a bad day?"

"More like a bad week," I answered. "Next lesson will be better, I promise."

I managed to get through the rest of the lesson, I'm not sure how, and was wheeling myself to his front door when my dad arrived to take me home in the van.

"How'd it go tonight?" my dad asked on the way home.

"Fair," I said.

My dad glanced over at me. "You've seemed pre-occupied lately," he said. "Is everything all right at school?"

Leave it to my dad to notice. He's really some-thing. I don't think I've ever known anyone as per-ceptive about people as he is. He can pick up somebody's off-mood a mile away. I guess it's the writer in him. Writers have to be sensitive people.

"Yeah," I said. "Everything's fine."

"What's wrong, Chelsey?" he asked.

"What makes you think something's wrong?" I asked.

"Mostly because of the way you stare off into space and can't talk to anyone at home for more than a minute. You seem to lose concentration. And then, there's the fact that you haven't started reading my book yet." He stole a sideways glance at me with a little smile.

"Oh, I'm sorry, Dad," I said. "I really do want to read your book, very much! In fact, I'll start it as soon as we get home."

"I'd guess you were in love," he said, "but you look too worried for that. Do you want to tell me about it?"

"Oh, Dad," I said. "I don't know. There's just a lot going on."

"At school?" he asked.

"Mostly, I guess," I said. "That boy dying at the basketball game really threw me."

"That was a hard thing for you to see," he said. "That'd throw anybody."

I just couldn't decide whether or not to tell him. Detective Evans wanted me to, but I know how Dad and Mom both worry about me. They'd insist on being with me everywhere, and as much as I love them, that would really be a drag. One handicap is enough. That would just make it harder to be on my own.

No, I guessed I wouldn't tell him.

"Thanks for asking, Dad, but I'm fine. Really."

He looked at me doubtfully. "Well, if you ever care to talk about it, you know where to find me."

"Right," I said and managed a smile.

Just then we turned a corner about a block from home. It was dark outside, but a streetlight shone brightly from the pole across the street from our house. I've always liked the way the light shines through the elm tree right next to it, casting leafy shadows along the sidewalk and street.

As we approached the driveway, I noticed a dark car sitting at the curb across the street. We passed right alongside, and I glanced down into the driver's seat. Someone was sitting there.

A man.

He turned to look up at me in the van, and I caught my breath.

As my dad pulled into the garage, I turned back to see the dark vehicle pull away from the curb quickly with a screech of tires and head off down the street.

"I wonder who that was?" my dad said, turning off the ignition.

I knew who it was. I had seen his face very clearly. Ron Whitehill. And he had been waiting for me.

I started looking for Jack the next morning as soon as the Bionic Bus dropped me in front of the school. It was a beautiful spring day, the air cool with a warm sun on my shoulders. Most of the kids were milling around outside waiting for the first bell, some sitting on the grass, others huddled in groups chattering noisily.

I spotted Jack leaning against the building. His face was tipped up toward the sun. His eyes were closed. Some of the kids watched me curiously as I approached him.

"Jack, I've been looking for you!" I said urgently.

He opened one eye, the way a cat does when it really doesn't want to be disturbed. Then he closed it again.

"Hi, Chels," he said. "Getting a start on my tan."

"Listen, I've got something important to tell you," I said.

"Shoot," he said lazily.

So I described what happened when I arrived home from my lesson, how I'd seen Ron's face and how he'd zoomed off down the street as soon as I saw him.

By this time, Jack had both eyes open and they were staring at me with increasing horror.

"Chelsey, are you *sure* it was Ron?"

"No doubt in my mind, Jack. None."

"He didn't take long to find you," Jack said. "He's probably been watching your house, learning your schedule, figuring out when and how to get to you."

I'd been trembling most of the night, and now it started all over again.

"Jack, I'm really scared," I said, trying to steady my voice. "I don't know what to do."

Jack put his arm around my shoulder and gave me a little hug. "Don't worry, Chels," he said. "I'll stick around you all the time. I won't leave you alone, except when you're in class or at home."

"Do you think I should call Detective Evans?" I asked.

"If you want to," Jack said. "Did you talk to your parents?"

"No," I said. "Maybe I should have. I was afraid they'd crowd me too much. You know."

"Yeah," he said. "Well, if you don't mind, I'll crowd you instead."

"Okay," I answered, feeling a little better.

"Chelsey," he said. "I've been thinking. I don't want to wait around for the police to do their work." I glanced at him, frowning, and he said, "Now just a minute. Listen to me."

He paused and kicked at a rock with his toe. "I've decided to do something right for once."

"What do you mean?" I asked.

"Well, Evans was really nice yesterday, you know? And I'm the best person to get information for this investigation anyway. I know how Mac's operates and I know both men involved. I could really help the police bring them in."

"Jack," I protested, "remember what Detective Evans said yesterday? He said for both of us to stay clear of Mac's. We're both in danger."

"Yes, but what if I could get hold of that little black book? And what if it's filled with evidence, like names and addresses and numbers of dollars paid for drugs?"

"But you said that book is locked up in Mac's drawer."

"What if I could get it?" he said with a sly look in his eyes.

"But how?" I asked bewildered. "How could you do that?"

Jack slipped a hand into his pocket and brought out a silver key. "This opens the back door at Mac's," he said.

I gasped. "How did you get that?"

He shrugged. "I work there, remember? I have a key so I can get in to wash the floor. Mac is almost always there, but what if I go at a time when he *isn't* there? Like tonight?"

I shook my head. "It's too dangerous, Jack. Don't try it. What if Mac or Ron decides to go back to the office when you're there? They'd kill you just like they killed Jerry."

"It won't happen," he said.

"But you don't *know* that," I said.

Jack paused a moment and stared into space. "Well, I'm going to do it tonight, anyway, Chels."

Jack had obviously made up his mind, and I wasn't going to change it. "Well, okay, Jack," I said. "But if you're going to do something this dangerous, you'll need some help. So I'm going with you."

He looked at me in astonishment. "You're going to help? How?" He glanced at my wheelchair.

"Do you think I can't help you?" I asked. "Just because I'm in a wheelchair?"

"Well, let's face it, Chels," Jack said, "you could really slow me down if I have to move fast."

He had a point, but I wasn't about to admit it.

"Well, what if I come along to stand guard? Come

on, Jack. I can't just sit at home, knowing you're out digging up evidence and maybe in danger. I want to come with you."

Jack looked at me doubtfully. "How could you get out of the house? You couldn't very well say to your parents, 'Well, I'm going out now. I'll be collecting proof that two men I know are murderers. Don't wait up!' " He smiled a little. "And I couldn't very well drag you out of your bedroom window. You need your chair."

I thought a moment. Jack was right. Getting out of the house would be the hardest part.

At least, that's what I *thought* would be the hardest part.

Suddenly I had an idea.

"I know!" I said. "We're making this too complicated! Why don't you just come over to my house tonight and ask me if I want to go for a walk? I only live about six blocks from Mac's."

"Six blocks?" Jack said. "That's a long way. It'd take us twenty minutes to get there."

"That's right," I said, disappointed. "And we'd have to get around Suicide Hill."

Suicide Hill is the steepest street in town. It's work for even hardy, healthy pedestrians to climb that hill, and very difficult for cars in the winter. It would be practically impossible for Jack to push me up that hill in my wheelchair.

"But we could take two extra blocks out of the

way and avoid the hill completely," I said. "Jack, I know it's a long way, but you need me to stand guard for you."

"*Stand* guard?" Jack said, smiling.

"Don't get smart," I said. "You know what I mean. You need my help."

Jack thought a moment. "Well, you've got a point," he said. There was a long pause. "You really think your parents would let you go out for a walk — with me?"

"Why not?" I wanted to know.

"I don't know," Jack said. Then he shook his head. "I guess I always expect the worst."

"Well, don't worry about it," I said. "Just come and meet them. I know they'll like you."

"Right," he said, kind of sarcastically. Then he paused again and his tone softened. "Okay, Chels. I'll be there for you at nine-thirty."

I took out a piece of paper from my notebook and began to scribble my address.

Jack reached over and squeezed my hand. "I don't need your address, Chels," he said. "I already know where you live." I looked up at him in surprise.

He shrugged and smiled that little smile of his.

Ten

"So what's he like?" my mother asked with a faint smile.

"Who?" I said, looking as innocent as possible.

"What do you mean, 'who'?" my mother said. "The boy who's coming here to take you for a walk."

"Oh. Well, he's nice."

"Tell us about him," she said.

I glanced over at my dad, who was gazing at me over the top of the evening paper. He ducked back behind it, pretending to read.

"What do you want to know about him?" I asked.

"Well, how about his name?" my mother said.

"Jack Smith," I said.

"Sounds like he made it up," my mother said. "How well do you know this boy?"

"He didn't make it up," I said. "That's really his name."

"I was just kidding," Mom said. "Is he in seventh grade?"

"No, he's in eighth."

"Ooooooh," my mom said, nodding. "An older man. I always liked older men, myself. Your dad is one, you know."

"Careful, Jenny," Dad mumbled from behind his paper.

"Mom," I said, "Jack is very nice, and I'm sure you'll think so yourself. You can meet him as soon as he gets here."

"Okay," my mom said cheerfully, apparently satisfied. She went back to her Lawrence Block novel.

Even though I sounded pretty cool to my parents, I wasn't feeling cool at all. First of all, Mom and Dad would have to meet Jack. I didn't know how they'd take to him. But that was the least of my worries.

What was I going to do when we got to Mac's? Would we really be in danger?

What a dope. Of course we'd be in danger. Mac and Ron had already killed once. What're two more murders?

Jack rang the doorbell at exactly nine-thirty.

"Well, he's prompt," Mom said, smiling, and headed for the door.

"Oh, I'll get that, Mom," I said and cut her off with my wheelchair.

I pulled the door open, and there he stood.

He looked great, as if we were really going out on a date or something instead of breaking into a pizza joint. Well, not exactly breaking in. He *did* have a key.

He was wearing Levi's and what looked to be a new button-down shirt, with a tie hanging loosely around his neck. The tie was green and went great with his hair.

"Hi, Jack," I said.

He nodded, grinning. "How're you doin'?"

"Come on in," I said.

He stepped inside and my parents came over to the door to meet him. They looked a little startled.

"Hello, young man," my father greeted him, putting out his palm.

"Hello, sir," Jack said politely and shook his hand.

"This is my mother," I said, turning to her. She was staring at the top of Jack's head. "Mom?"

"Oh, yes," Mom said, smiling vaguely, still staring. "Jack, it's very nice to meet you."

"Thank you," Jack said.

There was an awkward silence. Everyone stood like mannequins in a department store.

"Well," I said, "I guess we'll be going now. It's really a beautiful night, isn't it?"

The mannequins suddenly came to life.

"Oh — yes, it is," Dad said. "Well, you kids have fun now. But not too late, Chelsey. Tomorrow's a school day."

"Okay, Dad," I said and looked at him. I wondered for just a second if I would ever see him and my mom again.

Enough of that, I thought.

The door closed behind us, and Jack pushed me down the front walk.

"How do you think that went?" he asked. "I thought it went pretty well, didn't you? I didn't swear or anything."

I laughed. "You were great," I said. "But I think they about had a cow when they saw your hair."

"Yeah," he said. "I know."

We walked along in silence. Then he said, "You look pretty sharp, Chels. Not like you're sneaking into a murderers' den."

"I was thinking the same thing about you," I said.

"Well, we had to make it look good for your parents, right?"

"Right," I said.

After another long pause he said, "Maybe the next time, it'll be a real date."

I couldn't help smiling, but I didn't look at him.

"Okay," I said. Then a sobering thought came to me. "If we make it through this night."

"Stop worrying, Chels," Jack said. "Everything'll be okay."

"It's a good thing you're not expecting me to push you up Suicide Hill," Jack said a few minutes later. "It's really a monster."

"It sure is," I agreed.

We had to walk the two extra blocks to avoid the hill; the land flattened out pretty quickly on one side, and sloped up gently over four blocks instead of practically straight up in a two-block hill.

We'd been traveling for about fifteen minutes when Jack said, "Man, I bet I'm the only detective in the world with an assistant in a wheelchair. Makes it kind of hard to slip in and out of shadows, you know."

I turned to look up at him. "Well, I bet I'm the only detective's assistant in the world who has a boss with green hair. Makes it kind of hard to be inconspicuous, you know."

Jack grinned. "Yeah, we do make an eye-catching pair."

In another five minutes we could see Mac's Pizza half a block away, closed and locked up for the night. A light overhead illuminated a deserted parking lot at the side of the building. We stopped across the street, right in front of the restaurant. A parked car sat at the curb between Mac's and us. We stood in the shadow of a tall tree.

I'd enjoyed the walk so much I'd almost forgotten why we'd come. But as soon as I saw Mac's, all dark and sinister-looking, I began trembling all over. I hoped Jack didn't notice.

We were really going to do it. We were really going to collect evidence against Mac and Ron, a pair of killers. What if they came to the pizza joint before Jack got out of there? I didn't even want to think of that.

"Well, here we are," Jack said, rubbing the palms of his hands together. He reached into his jacket pocket and pulled out a flashlight.

"Yeah," I said and giggled a little. (I always giggle when I'm nervous. It's a dead giveaway.)

"Okay, Chels," he said. "You stay right here. I'm going inside."

"I'm going to wait for you next to the building," I said.

"No," Jack said. "You stay here. If I have to get out fast, I want you at least across the street."

"But I can't stand guard for you here," I said. "How would I let you know if anyone is coming?"

Jack was silent a moment and looked around him. His eyes fell on the parked car, and he quickly ran around to the far side of the automobile.

"Great!" he said. "The driver's window is open." I didn't understand. "Listen, if you see anyone coming, just scoot your chair down this driveway into the street and honk the car's horn. I'll hear it and get out of there fast. Okay? Then duck down behind the car, and I'll come and get you just as soon as I can."

"Okay," I agreed, but I couldn't control the shiver that suddenly whipped through my body.

"Hey, Chels," Jack said. "Are you scared?"

"No," I lied. "I'm just a bit cold."

He smiled at my fib. "Don't worry. It'll be okay. I'll be right back."

He squeezed my shoulder gently, then headed off across the street.

Eleven

I watched Jack from the shadows as he stepped up on the far curb and crossed the lighted parking lot next to Mac's. He disappeared behind the restaurant.

Without Jack there, I felt very alone, and all at once I became aware of everything around me. Every shadow, every little sound caused my imagination to play tricks with my mind.

The soft clicking together of branches above my head startled me.

It's only the wind in the trees, I told myself. *Relax*.

A sudden scurry in the bushes nearby sent my heart leaping into my throat. Then, moments later, I saw a small rabbit scamper across the lawn behind me.

Oh, hurry up, Jack, I thought.

And then I thought of my friend Jack inside Mac's, armed with nothing but a flashlight. Suddenly, it didn't seem so scary out here on the sidewalk, out in the open.

Jack was crawling around in the dark inside. Did he find the notebook? What was taking so long?

Then I remembered that Jack had said the notebook was locked up in Mac's desk drawer. Was Jack breaking into the desk? Wasn't that illegal? And if he got evidence by breaking into the desk, would the police be able to use it against Mac and Ron? Oh, why didn't I think to ask these questions before — before Jack took the risk of sneaking inside? Maybe all this effort and danger would be of no use.

A light flashed in my eyes from down the street, and I ducked a little in my wheelchair into the shadow of the tree. The headlights came closer until I saw the outline of an approaching van. It moved slowly, and I watched as it pulled into Mac's lot.

When it passed under the light, I could make out the letters on the side of the van. M—A—C—'S. Oh, no! It was Mac or Ron coming back to the restaurant!

And Jack was still inside!

My head spun, and I couldn't think of what to do. I just panicked. I wanted to scream to Jack and yell for him to get out of there, but for some reason I don't remember I stayed quiet.

Now, get in control, I finally told myself. I was

squeezing the arms of the Blue Streak as hard as I could.

The driver's door of the van swung open, and a man jumped down to the concrete. He stood in the shadow of the open door, and I couldn't make out who he was. I saw a flicker of light in the blackness surrounding him. The light snapped off, and his cigarette glowed bright and dim as he took a drag on it.

He took a step past the door, and the light hit his face.

Ron!

I thought of the way he sat in his car just last night across the street from my house, probably plotting my death while he was waiting for me to come home.

Then the passenger door opened, and out stepped Mac. Both of them were here. Both of them, killers. And now Jack was trapped inside!

That is, unless I could warn him in time for him to get out.

That's what Jack told me to do, to warn him, to blare the horn in the car.

Finally getting my head together, I spun my wheelchair around and down the driveway into the street. I had to honk that horn inside the parked car before Mac and Ron got inside! They were heading around the corner of the building now!

I wheeled up alongside the car.

Just as I was about to reach inside, a man loomed up out of nowhere and said, "Excuse me, young lady, could you move to the side a little? I need to get into my car."

Breathing hard, with my heart hammering at my ribs, I stopped and looked at him. I couldn't see his face very well; it was in shadows. I glanced back across the street and saw that Mac and Ron had disappeared.

Probably into the building. Probably to discover Jack rifling through drawers, storage shelves, and anything else he thought might be hiding evidence that would prove Mac's Pizza was a cover for drug dealing.

Feeling numb, I slowly moved my chair to the side and let the man get into the car. He drove off down the street, his taillights diminishing and finally disappearing into the night.

And I just sat there.

I must have sat for a full minute, wrestling inside my brain, trying to figure out what to do. I should have talked to the man who drove away in the car. I should have asked him to help, to go get the police.

Why didn't I? Some help *I* was. I'd begged to come with Jack, and I didn't even do the one thing I came for — warn him that Mac and Ron were on their way inside.

I don't know why I started across the street toward the restaurant. I didn't even think about it, and I sure didn't know what I was going to do when I got there. I only knew I couldn't just sit across the street and wait.

I had to wheel maybe thirty feet out of my way at the other side of the street to get to a driveway so that I could pull myself up onto the curb. Then I scooted along the sidewalk as fast as I could and crossed the parking lot.

A yellow glow was cast onto the grass at the back of the restaurant. That meant the lights were on inside the office. Where Mac and Ron were.

And where Jack was.

I continued around the side of the building until I could see the window where the light was coming from.

I was on grass now, and it was difficult moving in the wheelchair. But I tugged at the wheels as hard as I could, and slowly, slowly made my way over to the window.

Just next to the window was a big shrub that came almost up to my shoulder. I ducked down a little and pulled myself alongside it.

Then I peeked up and over the bush and into the lighted room.

Ron was standing in the middle of the room and Mac was sitting lazily in a chair with his feet propped up on the desk in front of him. They obviously hadn't seen Jack.

Where was Jack? I couldn't see him anywhere.

Then Mac got up, stretched, and taking a key out of his pocket, inserted it in the lock of the desk drawer in front of him. A puzzled look passed over his face as, without turning the key, he slid the drawer open.

His eyes widened and he began looking frantically through the drawer, muttering and then yelling to Ron.

I couldn't hear what he was saying, which was probably just as well. He looked furious.

Ron ran over to Mac and helped him ransack the desk, looking for whatever was missing.

The notebook! Jack must've gotten it! But where was Jack?

The two men began rummaging through boxes and shelves, searching all over the office.

Jack, where are you? I thought wildly. He hadn't come out of the building. I would've seen him.

Just then, I caught sight of something moving a little over in the corner of the room. Under a shelving unit.

A foot. It moved again.

Jack was in the office with them!

His foot moved again. He was hiding behind a large carton, curled up into a tight little ball. He'd become as small as he could make himself.

Ron was looking high and low and getting closer to Jack. I thought for a second of the game "Hot 'n' Cold" I used to play when I was little. Paula would hide something in her living room, and I'd try to find it while she gave me hints as to whether I was hot or cold, getting closer or farther away from the treasure.

Ron was getting very hot.

And so was I. My heart was pounding, pounding in my chest and I kept saying under my breath, "Oh, please, oh, please, don't let them find Jack!"

Ron approached the carton hiding Jack and shifted it a little to one side. I took a big breath and held it, afraid to look but afraid not to.

Then he slid it back into place, shaking his head. Mac stopped his searching and they exchanged a few words. Both men looked panicky and furious at the same time.

They knew their notebook had been stolen. The notebook with all the evidence against them.

They turned abruptly and headed for the door. I ducked down as low as I could behind the shrub.

The door swung open at the back of the building, the lights snapped off, and the men hurried out.

"We'll find him!" Ron said angrily. "We'll get that Smith kid before he gets to the cops. I'll shut him up good. Just like I did that Fields kid!"

"You do that!" Mac spat back at him. And I didn't hear the rest, as they hurried off into the night.

Twelve

So Jack was safe. For the moment, anyway.

I wheeled myself over to the office door just as he slipped outside.

"Jack!" I whispered loud enough for him to hear.

He whirled around, grinned, and pulling a little notebook out of his jeans pocket, held it up proudly.

"Got it!" he said.

"Jack, I'm so sorry I let you down!" I burst out. "I'm sorry I didn't beep the horn for you!"

"No problem," he said. "Good thing I heard them coming. Just in time. I snapped off my flashlight and dove behind the box as they came in the room."

"I couldn't signal to you," I said. "A man drove the car away just as I —"

"Hey, no problem, Chels," Jack said, taking hold of my chair and starting to move into the parking lot.

"We've got to hurry now. We've got to get this note-book to the cops."

"Jack," I said, "they know you took it. I heard Mac and Ron talking when they came out of the office. They're looking for you. Ron said he is going to — to kill you."

"I know," Jack said. "Don't worry, Chels. We'll get to the cops before they get to me."

"How're we going to get to the police station?" I asked him. "We can't walk from here, and the Bionic Bus stopped running at ten."

"I know," Jack said. "I've got it figured out. We'll get to a phone and call Detective Evans. I know where there's a phone booth, at the corner of Fifth and Market streets."

"But what if they see you?" I said. "Jack, didn't you hear me? They're out looking for you. They may even still be around in the neighborhood."

"That's why we've got to move it," Jack said, picking up speed. I'd never traveled so fast in my chair before.

Jack laughed and squeezed my shoulder, still jogging and pushing me along the walk.

"We did it, we did it!" He laughed again, and my heart did a little dance to hear him so happy. "We'll put those guys away, Chelsey, and they won't be able to hurt anyone ever again."

I felt good but at the same time very scared. We

wouldn't exactly be hard to spot from a passing van. I mean, we were moving under streetlights at ten-thirty at night, a fourteen-year-old boy with green hair, running along and pushing a blond girl in a wheelchair. And there was no crowd around to disappear into. And no shops open to hide in.

Sitting ducks, I thought.

Open targets.

"Jack, I see a van coming!" I squealed. "We've got to hide!"

The large round headlights were halfway down the block. Maybe it was Mac's van and maybe it wasn't. But we couldn't take the chance.

We were on a section of street with no overhead light. I glanced up. The streetlight was dead.

Maybe they hadn't seen us yet.

But they were about to. Their lights were almost on us. I looked around wildly for a place we could hide.

Then Jack shoved my chair as hard as he could, and we scooted behind the corner of an apartment building just as the van's headlights struck the brick wall.

I was as close to the wall as I could get, and Jack had plastered himself against the brick.

The van passed slowly.

It was Mac's all right.

And both men were inside.

They continued on their way, slowly but steadily, obviously searching. For Jack.

"Man, was that close!" Jack let out a long breath, leaning against the building.

"Jack," I said, "You'd better go on. Get hold of the police, and then send someone to come get me."

Jack shook his head. "No way," he said.

"Look," I said. "They're looking for *you* now. If they see you, you'll need to get away fast. And you know that you can't move fast if you're lugging me around."

"Shut up, Chels," Jack said.

"I really want you to go on," I said.

"I don't even hear you," he said.

"Jack?"

"Shut up."

We hurried along down the street, under the lights, into the shadows, back into the lights again. Dark, empty stores, parking lots, and an occasional house hustled past as we hastened toward the phone booth, now only half a block away.

I could see the booth. The blue and white telephone sign lit up a tiny piece of the night just at the top of Suicide Hill. The hill bent down so steeply on the other side that from where we were we couldn't see the sidewalk past the booth. The telephone appeared to be standing at the edge of the world. One step beyond, and we'd fall off into deep space.

We stopped at the half-opened door.

"Do you have a quarter for the call?" I asked Jack.

My heart sank. "I didn't bring my wallet. I didn't think about bringing money."

Jack shoved his hands into both pockets and brought them out empty.

He pounded a fist into the side of the steel structure and cursed softly. Then he let out an exasperated breath. "I'm sorry," he said.

"Wait!" I'd just remembered something. "My mother has always told me to keep an emergency quarter at the bottom of my wheelchair bag. I've never used it. I bet it's still there."

I whipped the bag off the back of the Blue Streak and thrust my hand in. I couldn't see well enough to look inside, but after a minute of groping through my junk I came up with a large coin.

"Ha!" I said. "Good old Mom." And I held it up for Jack.

He took it, grinning, and slid the booth door open. The light popped on and he dropped the quarter into the slot.

9-1-1. He paused. The quarter dropped into the change box — we'd forgotten 911 calls are free.

"Hello," he said then. "I have an important message for Detective Evans at the police station," he said. "This is Jack Smith. Tell him I've got some very important evidence for him. I'm with Chelsey, and we're at the corner of Market and Fifth —"

Jack never finished the call.

The line went dead.

That's because at that moment, a long, strong arm reached into the phone booth and ripped the receiver out of Jack's hand and then tore the wires out of the phone.

Thirteen

Ron grabbed Jack around the neck in a head-lock, slipped something out of his pocket, and snapped open a switchblade.

"Now you're going to come out real nice and not give me any trouble," he said, between clenched teeth.

"Jack!" I blurted out.

From behind me, a hand grabbed my shoulder and squeezed till it hurt.

"Shut up," Mac's voice growled at me and his other hand clamped over my mouth, muffling the cry of pain that was already a scream in my throat.

"Let her go!" Jack yelled, trying to tear away from Ron's grasp. Ron only tightened his arm around Jack's neck and stuck the point of the knife just under Jack's chin.

"If you don't settle down, Smith, you're going to

watch while I cut up your little girlfriend, and then you're next."

Jack stared at me with horrified eyes and stopped struggling.

"Come on," Mac said nervously. "Let's get out of here. Ron, put that knife away. Someone might see you.

Ron released his hold on Jack and moved to the van parked just in back of us in the street at the crest of the hill.

"Okay, Smith," Mac said, "let's have it."

"What?" Jack asked innocently.

"Look, punk," Mac said impatiently, "we know you've got the notebook, so just hand it over."

"Want me to pry it loose?" Ron asked Mac.

"Not here," Mac said, looking over his shoulder nervously. "Get them in the van. And make it snappy."

I slipped my hand down quickly and locked the wheels on my chair. It was the only thing I could think of to stall a second or two.

Ron grabbed Jack's shoulder roughly and shoved him toward the waiting van.

"Come on, girl, get going," Mac said, nodding toward the open van door.

I pretended to push my wheels. They didn't budge.

"Oh, I forgot I locked the wheels," I said.

I leaned forward as if I were studying the wheel lock.

"What's the problem?" Mac sounded edgy. "What's going on?"

"Jack," I called. "Remember when my wheels locked yesterday? How did you fix them? It was kind of tricky."

I looked at Mac. "I'm sorry," I said. "I really am. Jack can fix it right away."

Jack hesitated a moment, and then he stepped up the curb and crossed the sidewalk to my chair. "It's locked again?" He glanced down at me, his eyes questioning, and then leaned over my chair.

"It's way down here," I said loudly. Then I frantically whispered into his ear, "Climb on, Jack!"

Jack realized instantly what I had in mind, and he gave my chair a hard shove right over the edge of Suicide Hill just as I released the lock, then hoisted himself over the side of the chair and plopped right in my lap.

And we went careening down the sidewalk, away from the two men who wanted to murder us, but onto a roller coaster ride that could kill us just as dead.

Just like a roller coaster picking up speed on the biggest, grandest screamer hill at the amusement park, so did we — only there was no safe stop at the end.

In fact, I remembered with horror that the bottom of the hill opened onto a parking lot, and at the end of it was the river.

The concrete sidewalk whizzed past us, fading quickly in intervals as we sped out from under street-lights and into the dark patches of street, then into the light again.

I couldn't see anything in front of me except Jack's back, and I hugged him as tight as I could around the waist, while the world rushed past us at breakneck speeds.

Out of the corner of my eye I caught a glimpse of headlights in the street next to us.

"Jack!" I screamed. "They're here! They're following us!"

The sidewalk beneath us abruptly ramped into a cross street.

Car lights.

Blaring horns.

Squealing tires.

Me screaming.

A terrific sound of metal crashing metal.

And we sped by, leaving two smashed cars behind us.

I gripped Jack's waist as tight as I could.

We were unstoppable.

Out of control. Faster and faster.

Locking the wheels wouldn't work. We'd both be thrown.

Better ride it out.

I knew we must be close to the bottom. Close to the parking lot. And the river.

What were we going to do?

Suddenly, the cement beneath us leveled out, but we continued to speed out of control.

Into the parking lot.

No cars around. Too late at night.

But way, way too fast. Too fast to stop in time.

Sirens in the air.

"Jack!" I screamed. "Jump off! Jump off! Before we hit the river!"

I could see the river fast approaching. We'd never be able to stop.

"Jump off!" I shrieked again.

Jack took a flying leap and spun, nearly in midair, to catch the handle of my chair behind me.

I could hear his feet flapping along in back of me as my chair began to slow.

Slower.

Slower.

And finally stopped, right at the water's edge.

Tires screeched just behind us as Mac's van careened into the parking lot and sped toward us. It stopped in front of my chair.

Ron and Mac's doors were flung open, and the two men jumped out and rushed at us.

Ron made a lunge for Jack, and Mac grabbed hold of my chair. Jack took a swing at Ron, who ducked and seized Jack's arms and pinned them behind his back.

Sirens screamed in the air, and a police car charged into the parking lot.

It screeched to a halt, the doors flew open, revealing guns at the open windows, and a voice yelled, "Hold it right there!"

Mac and Ron released their grips on us.

And Detective Evans, still holding his gun in front of him, walked slowly toward us.

Fourteen

Yeah, so we made the front page. It was all pretty exciting.

Who am I kidding? Exciting? It was exhilarating! We were heroes!

And my parents invited Jack over for dinner the next week. Mom made my favorite: fried chicken, with mashed potatoes and squash.

Not that I could eat anything. I was pretty nervous sitting there with Jack on one side and my parents smiling and smiling and sneaking glances at his green hair and everything.

"So, Chelsey, how did you ever get the idea to escape down that hill, anyway?" Amy asked.

"That certainly was a big risk!" my father said.

"I don't know how I thought of it, exactly," I said. "I just knew we were dead if we got into that van."

"Chelsey's good in the crunch," Jack said, grinning at me. "You were real cool, Chels."

My parents looked at each other and my mother mouthed the word, "Chels?" Then they winked at each other.

"How did Evans know where you were?" my dad asked.

"I was able to give the operator just enough information before Ron tore out the wires for him to piece it all together. He knew we were in trouble," Jack said.

"Well, we're very grateful to you, Jack," my father said. "You saved our daughter from falling into the river."

"I don't even want to think about it," Mom said. "But I'll think about it long enough to second that thank you and offer you some angel food cake."

I wanted to talk to Mom, so I volunteered to help cut the cake in the kitchen.

"Well?" I said when we were alone and out of earshot.

"Well, what?" my mother asked, pretending not to understand.

"Well, what do you think?" I said. "I mean about Jack. And everything."

My mother smiled. "I like him," she said.

"Even his hair?" I asked.

"Hmmm?"

"His hair. His green hair," I said.

"Oh, that," my mom said. "I'd hardly noticed."

Then she looked at me out of the corner of her eye, and we both laughed.

"Chelsey, we like him, so relax," my mom said and planted a kiss on my nose the way she did when I was little.

Back in the dining room, over angel food cake and ice cream, we discussed what would happen to Mac and Ron.

"Well," Jack said, "I talked to Detective Evans this morning. Not only will they be charged with the drug dealing and the murder of Jerry Fields, but now they've added charges of assault, attempted kidnapping, and attempted murder."

"And we'll be very glad to testify!" I said.

"You bet," Jack said.

My dad sighed. "Where will it all end?"

"End?" Jack said, taking my hand. "Mr. Bernard, this is just the beginning of a beautiful friendship!"

GO

Gorman, Carol.

Chelsey and the
green-haired kid.

$11.01

DATE DUE	BORROWER'S NAME	ROOM NO.
	Tayton B.	
	Riki	
12	Jaime B.	8

GO

Gorman, Carol.

Chelsey and the
green-haired kid.